Afterlife can be read either as a single book in its own right, or as the last in a series of four, titled *Soul Survivor Life*.

The aim of the series is to explain the basics of Christianity and Christian living in down-to-earth, jargon-free language. The four books follow the pattern of life: birth, adolescence, mid-life crisis and death. The first, *Walking with a Stranger*, explores what it really means to become a Christian, who God is and how we can build a personal relationship with him. *My First Trousers* looks at the challenges and rewards facing us when we start going deeper with Jesus. The Christian life is not easy, however, and *Weeping Before an Empty Tomb* asks how we cope when the going gets tough. The final book, *Afterlife*, is about facing the future, in particular death, heaven and eternity.

Mike Pilavachi is the founder of Soul Survivor and pastor of Soul Survivor, Watford. Craig Borlase is a free-lance writer. They have previously written two other books together, *Live the Life* and *For the Audience of One* (both Hodder Christian Books).

Afterlife

Facing the Future with God

Mike Pilavachi with Craig Borlase

Hodder & Stoughton
LONDON SYDNEY AUCKLAND

First published in Great Britain in 2000

10 9 8 7 6 5 4 3 2 1

British Library Cataloguing in Publication Data
A record for this book is available from the British Library

ISBN 0 340 73537 6

Typeset by Avon Dataset Ltd, Bidford-on-Avon, Warks

Printed and bound in Great Britain by
Clays Ltd, St Ives plc

Hodder & Stoughton Ltd
A Division of Hodder Headline
338 Euston Road
London NW1 3BH

To Elvira and Janet, our mothers.
We would not be here without you!

Contents

Acknowledgements

I would like to thank my friends at Soul Survivor who, when I felt like I was sinking, jumped in to save the drowning man. To Liz, who not only read the manuscript and made her usual wise comments but also cancelled my appointments on a couple of days and did not tell me until the night before. To Martyn Layzell, Carole Japtha and Neil Pearce, for their helpful suggestions and comments. To Jonathan Stevens, for his servant heart, enthusiasm and efficiency. To J. John, who has once again proved an invaluable honorary research assistant. There has not yet been an occasion when I have popped round to the Johns for coffee and not left with bags full of books, pamphlets and transcripts of past J. John sermons to help me on my way. To Matt and Beth Redman, the drama of whose lives keeps me entertained and anxious in equal measure. Let's hope the little one gets to lead a quieter life. Some hope!

To Ben Morrison, 'my soultimer', who has been a fantastic research assistant. To David Moloney, our editor at Hodder – thanks for your patience and continual flexibility, especially when it came to the deadlines. Last but by no means least, to Craig Borlase, whose friendship is a joy to me and whose writing skills never cease to amaze me. Thank you, little ones!

Introduction

In preparing to write this book I've read two books on angels, three books on Jesus' Second Coming, two more on death and various other leaflets, articles and backs of cereal packets. In the hope of coming up with something interesting to say about this most peculiar of subjects I trawled through such a variety of texts that I wound up not only confused, but enlightened, amazed and queasy all at the same time. You see, when it comes to death, not only are the vast majority of us in the West a bit slow when it comes to thinking about it, but we Christians also have the peculiar habit of embracing between us the most astoundingly diverse set of beliefs. Recently within the space of a couple of days I heard two Christian speakers give passionate yet totally opposing arguments about the very heart of Christian thought on the afterlife and things eternal: one believed that the Second Coming was just around the corner while the other was convinced that it could take both many events to unfurl and countless decades to pass before Jesus' return.

Now, of course the fact that there's a whole load of debate and difference of opinion within the Church shouldn't really be much of a surprise to anyone who has spent more than five minutes in a church council meeting, but something about this situation struck me as interesting. It's not that our beliefs can be so different that got me; it was the fact that when I stopped to ask myself what I thought about it, I realised that I really wasn't sure. In fact, when it comes to the whole thing of the Second Coming, the make-up of heaven and the future of mankind – and I probably ought to be embarrassed to admit this – it had been a while since I'd really got stuck into it. We'll go into reasons why this might be so later on in the book, but for now – to start things off gently – let's check out the landscape.

When it comes to what happens when we die, there's a wholesale fascination that runs through almost every aspect of contemporary culture like 'BRIGHTON' through a stick of rock. As with my two opposing speakers, for us Christians, things can begin to get a little muddy, but for the average bloke in the pub, the picture that enters their mind when the word *heaven* is mentioned might be reasonably clear: harps, clouds and all that. Others might opt for a fairly firm belief that what follows death is nothing more than nothingness. Christians, on the other hand, have it tough. We've got a book stuffed full of images that occasionally would seem more at home in a *Dungeons and Dragons* game, with material that has prompted theories and beliefs as diverse and confused as you could possibly imagine. Depending on what church you visit you might hear that heaven is a physical place, a spiritual state or that it exists already. Some choose to play it down while others like nothing better than to spice up a bland sermon with a few trouser-soiling examples about just exactly how you might be spending eternity should you fail to get things right this time around. It's confusing. I'm confused, and even after all my research, I think I'm only slightly better off. Never having let a little ignorance get in the way of things, however, I shall continue.

As the final book in the series, *Afterlife* takes a look at death. We'll examine theories and ideas about what things will look like for us once we're on the other side, as well as taking a slightly more sideways glance at how the concept of 'dying' translates into one of the most important aspects of the Christian life – sacrifice. We'll split the subject down the middle, with the literal biblical stuff on one side and the more personal lot on the other. There's far more to death than meets the eye, and hopefully we'll end up living stronger – if not longer – lives at the end of it.

While I'm not one for rules, we need to get a couple of things straight before beginning, particularly with regard to the concept of what happens to each of us after we've shuffled off this mortal coil. The key to any study/argument about life after death is not to get bogged down in speculation about whether it will take place on earth or in heaven or whether there will be sex there. Forget whether Jesus will be blond, black or fond of thrash-metal-hardcore-country dancing, the key is to remember that afterlife is life with God in all its fullness. It means seeing him face to face and, as Paul says in 1 Corinthians 13, now we see in part, then we will see face to face and we will know as we are known. If we really want to prepare for the kingdom to come the best thing we can do is to get used to living that way now. We all need to get to know the author of life while we're here. After all, he's the one who transcends and overpowers death.

One of my favourite countries to visit is South Africa. In fact, I'm going there in just two weeks' time and I can't wait. I haven't always felt this way, though; before my first visit to South Africa I was quite apprehensive and uncertain, mainly because I knew no one from that country. Now I have many friends there. My friends are waiting for me. It's the same with heaven. My friend Jesus is waiting for me. The more I get to know him the less apprehensive I will be. I have often found that those who know God the best are those who fear death the least.

We often can get our focus wrong, both when it comes to heaven and God in general. Because we're fond of entertainment and shy of hard graft with little reward, we can often find ourselves getting well into seeing God work or having him do something spectacular in our lives but switching off at the thought of working at getting to know him better. We often would rather be a spectator than a player, and when it comes to God this can lead to an unfortunate lack of balance in our relationship with him.

The same can be said of our approach to the afterlife; we love the thought of all that time and goodness, but are unprepared for the prospect of being quite that close to him. If we really are keen to think about and prepare for the next life, I would suggest that instead of worrying about the travel arrangements it's far better to get on with continually building on our relationship with God. Instead of merely coming to him like children, eagerly looking in his hands to see what gifts he has for us today, we need to be prepared to look into his face, to learn to recognise and appreciate him. The more we learn about Jesus, getting to know him, absorbing ourselves in him and gazing into his face, the more we will long not for death, but for what comes after it.

As Christians we get glimpses of the afterlife right here on earth. At one stage some people asked Jesus where the kingdom of heaven was. He told them that to try and plot it on a map was pointless for the simple reason that the kingdom of heaven is to be found within us. What did he mean? The kingdom of heaven is within us when Jesus, the king of heaven, makes his home in us. When I became a Christian, Jesus by his Holy Spirit came to live in me. Jesus was saying that the first thing we need to look for when we are searching for the kingdom, is not a physical place but a person (see Luke 17:20–21). You simply cannot define heaven without focusing on Jesus, for he is what it is all about.

We're fond of teasing ourselves by wondering whether we will recognise each other in heaven. For what it's worth I think we will be able to; we will have resurrection bodies just in the same way that Jesus does and did when he rose in bodily form from the dead. It does seem as though we will live on a new earth, one that will be redeemed and reclaimed, where all the effects of pollution and unnatural corrosion will be wiped clean. We will live as we were meant to live, on the earth as God intended it.

Much of this comes from the book of Revelation, and alongside these facts can be found the most obscure and figurative pieces of prose in the whole Bible. But if you manage to get to the end of the book you will see that more than it being about beasts covered in eyes or scrolls, horsemen and virgins, it is actually about Jesus. There is the most wonderful passage in chapter 22 verses 4 and 5:

> They [the servants of the Lord] will see his face, and his name will be on their foreheads. There will be no more night. They will not need the light of a lamp or the light of the sun, for the Lord God will give them light.

God himself is light, and he will call us home. It matters less where that home is or how it will look, and matters more who will permeate its every corner; the answer is God himself. He is the afterlife.

1

The D Word

Death: the final frontier. Our bravest have
conquered Everest, our most intelligent have placed
their fellow humans on the moon. Our most
beautiful are celebrated the world over and our
history books are littered with tales of excellence
and exception. Scientists have broken through
medical barriers that only a handful of years ago
were considered immovable. Barely a week goes by
without an announcement of a new development
that promises to shape the way the world will be
tomorrow. 'The future is now' we tell ourselves,
chests swollen with pride as we sample the air of
the new dawn of the millennium. Evolution or not,
there are plenty of us who believe that we are one
seriously impressive species. 'Well done, human

beings,' we say to ourselves, 'you're coming along nicely.'

But deep down we know that all the perfect smiles and jaw-droppingly impressive achievements in the world cannot alter the fact that there is still one thing that we cannot overcome. The clock is ticking for each of us, and while the diets and exercise may be able to slow it down, none of us can put off the inevitable: one day we will die, and what happens after that is something many of us would rather not think about.

At the end of the day, each of us will face an ending. It doesn't matter about wealth, health or social standing, death is the final frontier we simply cannot avoid. It unites us all, bringing together the rich and the poor, the famous and the forgotten, the foolish and the wise.

The fundamentally democratic rule of 'one person, one death' applies today as much as it did when life expectancy was well below fifty years and a common cold could be fatal. No matter how hard we try to drag things out, in the long run our death rate is 100 per cent; we're all going to die.

It's kind of odd then, that such an important and universal subject should be such a taboo. After all, if we're all going to end up the same, shouldn't we be able to talk about it a little more? But we can't quite seem to be able to manage to overcome our fear and find out how others feel. As far as conversation goes, death is off the menu. It's the 'd' word; the subject that's best avoided, like politics and religion.

I found this out for myself when I was seven years old. My first pet had just died – an obese hamster by the name of Gunter (I was into German football when I named him). Gunter was great and his death was a bit of a blow. However, not being told otherwise, I saw no reason why the mere fact that he had stopped breathing should separate us. As a matter of fact, now that his body had stopped working, carrying him around in my pocket during the day was far less trouble than when he was alive (he had had a very weak bladder, you see). And so he remained in my coat pocket for the first few days after his passing. I would stroke him as I walked along and he, well, he would just lie there, eyes wide open and claws outstretched as if contemplating the very make-up of the universe itself.

One day – a while later – it was my turn to step up to the front of the class and grasp my fifteen minutes of fame in a round of Show and Tell. I was excited and couldn't wait to bring Gunter out and tell the whole class about our new-found friendship. I stood at the front – chest out, shoulders back – and went into intricate detail about my life with Gunter. I told them about the day that I bought him, about the naming ceremony, the joy of playing with him every day and the trauma of seeing him get caught in the food processor while my mother was making bread. (Thankfully he stood out well against the flour and a near crisis had been averted.) I must admit I was doing pretty well and could tell from the faces beaming back at me that they knew exactly how great a hamster Gunter was.

I was therefore surprised that when I came on to the subject of his death that my fellow classmates failed to share my excitement. For me, Gunter's passing had been a wonderful thing. To them, it was a horror story. As I plunged into ever more intricate detail about how Gunter breathed his last (no time to tell it now, but it involved a trail of Brazil nuts and a faulty sandwich toaster) the tears began to flow from my audience. In a desperate attempt to convey that it had not been a tragedy but a wonderful new dawn, I pulled Gunter from out of my coat pocket and ran around the room waving his flat, branded and criss-crossed body under my colleagues' noses. There was chaos. I ended up with lines and Miss Jones's nerves never did seem quite the same again. Death, I found out, is not best introduced to the classroom.

Of course, over the years I developed a much more suitable and anglicised approach to death. Not only did I stop talking about it but I also stopped thinking about it. Like most of us I put it to the back of my mind, quarantined from the rest, buried deep down until it had to be faced when some other Gunter met the grand sandwich toaster of life.

Apart from my hamster story, there aren't many better examples of how keen we are to avoid the subject of death than in our language. We wrap it up in all sorts of fluffy phrases in a desperate attempt to make it easier to swallow. 'He's passed away' we gently sigh or talk about how 'she's gone to a better place'. People are 'at rest' or have 'moved on'. We even apply the same rule to our animals, choosing to declare that they are 'put to sleep' instead of killed or put to death.

Today we have less experience of death than we ever did. While there might be fewer people being born in the Western world, we're managing to hang on that little bit longer before we finally do get around to kicking the bucket. These days it's getting increasingly unusual for young people to experience the death of a close friend or family member; one hundred years ago a teenager may well not only have lost the odd grandparent, but perhaps a parent and a sibling or two. Back in the twenty-first century it is precisely because of this lack of experience that many of us are becoming increasingly ill-equipped to deal with death.

At the same time we're fascinated by it; from TV to the cinema, fiction to art, we just cannot seem to keep away from it. For many of us this is the nearest that we get to death. Whether it's comic book violence or morbid fascination, the 'd' word has also become a billion-dollar industry, and the tills keep on ringing. But this type of approach to death has changed things for us. It has sanitised it, cleaned it up and made it far easier to swallow. In films it's not unusual to get into double figures with on-screen deaths during the duration of a picture – but this is nothing new; after all, Shakespeare was well into a bit of bloodbath in his day, as the final moments of *Hamlet* make clear. It's not just about quantity, it's about attitude. When James Bond pumps a slug from his Walter PPK into a baddie, we don't think twice about the significance of the event. In the film *Austin Powers, International Man of Mystery* it is put so well as the wife of a recently killed henchman of Dr Evil turns to camera and suggests that no one stops to think about the family of an evil tyrant's henchman. Freshly cleaned up and rendered suitable for family viewing, we clock up an astonishing number of on-screen deaths, and by the time they are sixteen, the average American has seen 18,000 murders on TV. Among a UK audience, the figures are equally shocking.

Our cartoon attitude to violence spills over to our perspective on war and human tragedy. The pictures that were beamed back from Kosovo and Chechnya held our attention for about as long as they could, but sooner or later the channel got flicked, the kettle put on and we returned to the business of getting on with our lives. It's such a familiar sight to all of us that death these days doesn't seem to be quite what it was, and viewing the end of someone's life just doesn't seem to be enough to hold our attention.

But despite this easy attitude there have been many studies that have pointed to death as being the main source of worry among young people today. The thought of a premature death, of dying before our time, is often almost too much to bear. It's not hard to get your head around it either, as with the proliferation of nuclear weapons, the reports of advances in chemical and biological warfare and the ease with which conflicts flare up into full-scale stand-offs, death can sometimes seem just around the corner. We have the capacity to destroy ourselves many times over, and with the breakdown of the Soviet Union, the arrival of India and Pakistan to the list of nuclear countries and the likelihood that the same applies to Israel, Iran and others in the area, many are worried that it is only a matter of time before some nutter finds his finger on the trigger.

Not only that, but there's the very real prospect that it won't even take a nuclear holocaust to finish our planet off; that we're doing quite a nice job of destroying the planet ourselves, thank you very much. The slow progress of ozone depreciation, pollution and global warming march us on towards a fate the full horror of which few of us have even begun to comprehend.

Then there are the new diseases that have come onto the scene over the last few years. Despite the warnings, HIV/AIDS is on the increase and cancer looks set to continue to baffle scientists well into the next couple of decades. A recent report by the Cancer Research Campaign suggested that cancer now hits four in every ten of the British population. Ironically doctors put this down partly to the fact that we are living longer. Instead of getting struck down by the killers of old such as pneumonia and septicaemia, we face an old age punctuated by the horrors of lung, breast, bowel and prostate cancer. Despite this, however, the death rates from cancer are dropping, thanks to advances in technology for treatment and detection. Still, the fact that many of us might be able to rate our own chances of making it through to a peaceful and natural death at the end of a long life may be some comfort, but what about our children; do they really stand a chance from all the rest of the killers that look set to darken future horizons?

Yet many of us seem to have such interesting and occasionally bizarre views on death that sometimes I find it hard to see the connection between what we imagine happens to us on the other side of life and the increasingly desperate-looking reality that has been described above. It wasn't that long ago that we all were treated to Mr Glenn Hoddle's views on exactly what was what and who would be in line for what in the life after this one. Thanks, Glenn. He's not alone, though, as there are plenty of others out there who share equally sanity-free ideas on the afterlife. Often a fine blend of Eastern mysticism, New Age focus and morality-lite pleasantries about 'being a good person', these views often touch on reincarnation, and for many it comes down to believing in something that simply makes them feel good.

Of course, these people are not in the minority; there's a huge hunger out there for understanding and a sense of purpose. From spiritualists and mediums to the use of Ouija boards and Tarot cards, people are prepared to go to great lengths to find out how the story ends.

In 1999 cinema-goers were treated to the ultimate horror movie, *The Blair Witch Project*. There was no blood, no on-screen violence and no traditional horror – just suspense as the film lived out our most common anxieties; that there is an unseen force out there which we don't understand, a force that will end our lives. The fear of the unknown is so great that for many viewers, the film was almost too much to bear. Interestingly the film was praised for its astonishingly low budget – costing just US$60,000 to make. The marketing bill wasn't quite as slimmed down, however, as in excess of $20 million was spent promoting the film.

Lots of us are scared about death and few could claim to fully understand it. Many are searching for answers, and I believe that the Christian faith provides something that is worth more than all the answers and all the theories on offer. It's called *hope*, but don't think I mean some kind of flimsy, fluffy hope, the sort based more on nice and cuddly feelings. The hope that comes prepacked for everyone who turns towards Christ is firm, based on reality and rooted in the eternal goodness that is God. Just take a look through the Bible and you will see how Jesus preaches a message that explains what it means to live a life that is not affected by death. Jesus redefined life and death, bringing them back on track and helping us to view them not as polar opposites, with life at the good end and death at the bad. Instead he taught us that life is made up of little deaths, that in learning how to follow him we would look beyond our own lives. At the heart of Christianity is the most upside-down death of all; Jesus on a cross. In dying Jesus took on himself the punishment for our sin. In rising from the dead three days later, he rewrote the rule book; death has lost its sting. We'll find out just how right this is throughout this book, but first it might be wise to take a stroll around the grand supermarket of life and see what they've got on a special offer in the death department.

Life and death can be hit-and-miss affairs. No matter how grand our lives, how great our achievements or well-known our exploits, death can often turn the tables. Of the great thinkers of the last century, Albert Einstein was probably the greatest. But when he died, his final words died with him. His nurses didn't speak German and so the final chapter of the man's story was left incomplete. Then there was Alfred Nobel; his life was dedicated to the discovery and perfection of dynamite. When by accident someone published his obituary before his death, Mr Nobel came face to face with the stark reality that his life had been about nothing more than perfecting the art of killing people. This sparked a full-on 180 degree turn and he altered his will to set up the Nobel Peace Prize, rewarding those who made great contributions to prolonging and enhancing life instead of destroying it.

Rock-and-roll's speeding highway is littered with stories of fast-living stars and celebs. 'Live fast, die young, leave a good looking corpse' so they say, and there are plenty taking the advice. From James Dean's fatal ride to Kurt Cobain's descent into the world of heroin and guns, we've developed a taste for this type of ending. We like our teen idols to go out in a blaze of glory. I mean, who hasn't felt a twinge of embarrassment as yet another dinosaur of rock fails to age gracefully on a trout farm but chooses instead to rock out with their zimmer frame in public? Mick Jagger's still at it, as are the front half of Led Zeppelin and dear old Cliff Richard. Generally these ageing hipsters don't have an easy ride of it in the public eye, and perhaps there is something about their highly visible struggle to be considered young way beyond the time when their grandchildren have learnt to drive that we all find vaguely embarrassing. Ending your career the way of Jimi Hendrix, Janis Joplin, Richie Manic or Jim Morrison helps keep you forever young in the land of pin-ups and rock legends.

But there's one who was the daddy of them all, out-consuming the others while alive and upstaging the rest after death. Of course I'm talking about Elvis, the man who was reported to have more drugs than Superdrug inside his body when the post mortem was carried out. He had a taste for burgers, pills, bourbon and handguns, not to mention the cat suits, capes and ballooning physique. In his heyday he was absolutely massive, but the exploitation of a crooked manager and a number of bad career choices left him facing a mixed reaction. Only a reincarnation as 'the Comeback Kid' and a string of gigs in Vegas helped him end on something of a high note. In terms of status, however, things got better for Elvis once he was dead. These days it seems like he cannot put a foot wrong.

Across the globe fans believe that his passing was their cue to celebrate his life in all manner of ways. First came the obsessive collectors, people who turned rooms and houses over to shrines of the man they called *The King*. Of course, this was helped by the fact that every money-minded souvenir producer jumped on the bandwagon after the singer's death, flooding the market with everything from Elvis plates and Elvis rugs to Elvis toilet-roll holders and Elvis condoms (I kid you not). Then came the impersonators, crooning and 'thangyouvermuch'-ing their way through the grand sequined jump suit of life. Here in the UK, Elvis-look-alike Gary Jay broke the world record for non-stop singing of Elvis's hits. He managed to score a whopping ten hours without a break, swivelling his way through more than a hundred of the greatest numbers.

For others, merely looking and sounding like their hero isn't enough, and every year fans gather at various locations (usually Graceland in Memphis being the main one) to celebrate the anniversary of Mr Presley's death. Putting their own unique twist on the man's style, it's not uncommon to witness all manner of Elvis impersonators on 16 August. There are Viking Elvises, Japanese Elvises, even an Indian Elvis, named Elvis Singh. This fine chap wearing a turban and excessively long sideburns has been known to croon: 'I don't do drugs, I don't drink bourbon, all I wanna do is shake my turban.'

But being an icon after death doesn't get much better than the lengths to which some Elvis fans have gone to; setting up their own church, The First Presleyterian Church of Elvis the Divine. Most aren't quite sure what they believe, but rumour has it that communion comes in the form of a Big Mac and double chocolate shake.

Moving back to reality, one of the great messages of Christianity is that in Jesus Christ we can have eternal life, made possible through Jesus' triumph over death. Yet, it strikes me as being quite odd that we use this message of eternal life as a selling point for people in and around our contemporary culture. Take a look around and it's plain to see that there are plenty of people within society who are continually debating how to end this life. Euthanasia, excess and a single-minded commitment to live for the moment don't seem to be particularly strong indications that news of a next life after this will go down too well.

Despite that, I believe that the eternal life Jesus offers is worth focusing on. I don't believe it's right to focus on quantity (after all, most people would agree that an infinity of anything is bound to get boring after a while), but instead we ought to be chatting about the quality of eternal life. You see, what Jesus offers is a life free from pain, and a life that goes even further; a life in the presence of God himself. Now that's got to be a hit.

'It's not that I'm afraid
to die. I just don't want to be
there when it happens.'
Woody Allen

'I am ready to
meet my maker, but whether my
maker is prepared for the great
ordeal of meeting me
is another matter.'
Winston Churchill

'I don't mind dying, it's just that
one is a little stiff the next
morning.'
Woody Allen

'I thank my God
for graciously granting me the
opportunity of learning that death
is the key which unlocks the door
to our true happiness.'
Wolfgang Amadeus Mozart

2

Life Is Made Up of Little Deaths

Before we get on to having a look at what lies in store for us on the other side of the funeral parlour, I propose we take a couple of chapters out to have a look at how death plays a part for each of us while we are very much alive. Looking at the subject, it seems clear to me that it isn't just limited to the obvious. Sure, on the one hand death is all about a decomposing/eternal life/plaque on a park bench type of thing. On the other hand, however, surely there's a bit of it that also affects life itself. We'll look at how to deal with grief and bereavement in the next chapter, but it also occurs to me that life itself – strangely – is made up of deaths; there is death at the end of life and there are deaths throughout it. It's not only when we breathe our last that we come face to face with death, but throughout our time on earth, almost from day one.

Each of us has a genetic blueprint, right? Well, in each of those blueprints can be found the code that may point to the closing chapters of our earthly destiny – high blood pressure, cholesterol or whatever. It's long been known that once we enter our third decade our bodies begin their slow decline as the creation of new cells is outnumbered by the level at which the others are dropping off. Sorry if all this sounds a bit depressing, but there is a point to it all. There's more to life being made up of death than merely cell-degradation and all that; death is much more than a physical thing, it is an emotional one as well. To say goodbye to a friend is to die a little death, to see an ambition finally become an impossibility is a little death. To lose a job or to move house will take us along the path of separation and ending, even if it might not necessarily include grief.

But for Christians there's something even more significant about a life full of small deaths. Following Christ means walking in his footsteps, and it doesn't take a genius to work out that his was a story marked at every turn by acts of selflessness and humility. Throughout his life, Jesus communicated a potent message about the need for people to follow his lead and put their own priorities and preferences second to his greater will.

If you're fond of Christian jargon you could call this *dying to self*. What a repulsive term. I can hardly think of anything less attractive. Thankfully Jesus fleshed the idea out a little, exclaiming at one point: 'If anyone would follow me, let him deny himself, take up his cross and follow me.' At another instant he suggested that 'if anyone seeks to gain his life he will lose it, but he who loses his life, for my sake and the gospel, will find it'. Maybe calling 'dying to self' repulsive was a bit strong; Jesus was pretty clear about things and it's obvious even from these two verses that he has a slightly different take on death from ours. Where we might get offended at the thought of having to die to anything – after all, we're *alive*, aren't we? – Jesus saw life as something different. Actually, he saw death as something different; not the horrendous ending that many of us fear. Instead death was something to be welcomed, to be embraced and ultimately to be conquered. For Jesus, death was a way of life.

Considering that we are a generation who live for the moment, seek pleasure wherever it might be found and who hope to extend life to the max, Jesus' words are strangely relevant. You might think me a fool for suggesting such a thing; after all, how on earth can two such opposite ideas ever be compatible? But I tell you that they can, that it is possible to get the most out of life at the same time as embracing the idea of self-sacrifice. The answer to a 100 per cent full life is not found in a pill, a boutique or that authentic East Asian travelling experience. The answer – according to God – is death. It's not only possible, it's vital.

Just the day before writing this chapter I visited my sister-in-law in hospital. She'd just given birth to her first child, a beautiful 3.5 kg girl called Emily. To be honest my sister-in-law was fairly spaced out from all the emotional and physical demands placed on her by the birth, and I knew that she was wondering about how she would cope as a first-time mother. She told me that she was scared that she wouldn't turn out to be a good mother, that she wasn't ready for all the challenges and changes that lay ahead. She knows even now that from the birth onwards – as well as being filled with an immeasurable joy – she will have to make some hefty sacrifices for little Emily. She might put to death perhaps the idea of buying that better house, going on that holiday or having that leisure time. For the first year or two she's most definitely going to have to put to death any idea of getting a regular and complete night's sleep. How can she do this? Because she loves her baby. The conclusion that we can draw from this is obvious; we are all happy to make sacrifices – even big ones that scare us senseless – for someone that we love.

There are plenty of other examples of sacrificial

love leading on to little deaths, the ultimate being Jesus himself. His life as described in the first four books of the New Testament is an astounding display of a series of smaller deaths and sacrifices leading to the most costly and important death of all. Following him means that we Christians need to understand that there's a tasty little paradox existing at the heart of life: the way to find real life, real joy and real fulfilment is to let go the fierce grip which we have on our own lives. The way to find fulfilment is through sacrifice for God and for others. Easy to say, hard to do.

When it comes to God that might mean – as we have covered in other books – offering him a sacrifice of praise, giving him our best and loving him even when it hurts. Living a life for God means realising that our life actually belongs to him rather that ourselves. Paul got it so right when he wrote in Philippians 1:21 'for me to live is Christ and to die is gain'. What does that mean? Paul had discovered that his life had been turned upside down and inside out by God himself. It was no longer about his own ambitions but being ambitious for the kingdom. He learnt to put his own motives and desires second, choosing instead to put God's agenda in front of his own. Millions of Christians have come across the same truth: that there's more to life than the here and now. Living it for God means that we are able to make the kind of sacrifices that would be almost unthinkable if we believed that there was nothing to come after this life. We Christians can see it all in context – God has created us, is calling us home and wants us to bring along as many guests as we can find.

As Paul discovered, we all need to live a lifestyle that's in step with the rest of the kingdom, consulting God and following him every step of the way. Living a kingdom lifestyle means recognising that he is God of our wallets as well as of our hearts. Surely the man who gave everything for us, the one who laid down his life for ours and who demonstrated how to live, deserves not only our full attention but our most radical commitment as well. We need to ask Jesus how he wants us to live in the light of the poverty that blights the majority of the world's population. How does he want us to live in response to the state of the environment? Perhaps we ought to be thinking about spending that little bit more on fairly traded products rather than the sometimes cheaper produce of less ethical companies. Perhaps we ought to think about where we bank in the light of the issues surrounding Third World debt. Perhaps we ought to consider the power of the vote and start mobilising those around us to influence those in a position to bring about change.

The other side of living a sacrificial life is to follow Jesus' model and live it for others. Take Mother Teresa of Calcutta, for example. She lived for the poor, turning from fame and wealth and choosing instead to care for those too poor to secure for themselves a dignified death. She found Jesus in the poor, following the trail of poverty, chastity and obedience. Then there's Jackie Pullinger – a British woman who has spent years working alongside drug addicts and gang members inside Hong Kong's Walled City. She boarded a ship from England with a one-way ticket and left behind her family, friends and financial security purely because she believed that God had told her to. There are hundreds, even thousands, of these stories about people who have given up all they had simply to follow Jesus, some even taking it to the point of death, giving their lives for the cause of the King. Many of them can be found in Foxe's *Book of Martyrs*, a fat book listing many of those who died for their belief in Christ in Europe up to the middle of the sixteenth century. Sacrifice, it would seem, is not dead and buried, but alive and well.

Here in the comfy West, being martyred can seem to us like a distinctly remote possibility, but it happens – if not on our doorstep then at least in other parts of the world. Would we be willing to take it all the way? Would we be willing to make the ultimate sacrifice? For most of us these questions are so far removed from our reality that they seem totally hypothetical. After all, how can we truly answer if the nearest we might come to death for a cause is stubbing our toe when rushing to turn the TV on?

But there is one way to find out whether we're on the right track. Are we living a life that is more than just peppered with little deaths? Are we giving up our will for God's? Jesus in the Garden of Gethsemane went through a deliberation prior to a sacrifice: 'May this cup pass from me . . . but not my will but yours be done.' That was him denying himself, taking up his cross, big time. Will we do the same? Chances are that it will be a less dramatic and final act that we are agreeing to, but will we go along with it all the same? It might be some cash that we would rather keep a hold on for ourselves – will we give it away? It might be someone that we really don't like hanging out with but who values our company nevertheless – will we put our own discomfort second and have them round?

There are all sorts of possibilities for sacrifices, yet sometimes it can be easier to imagine ourselves making the large heroic sacrifices – the ones that bring us widespread praise and attention – than it is to actually say yes to making the little, anonymous and unglamorous sacrifices that we face on an almost daily basis. Face facts, nobody's going to want to read a book made up of gloriously victorious stories of how we managed to listen to someone who bugged us or cleaned up after someone was ill. No, we much prefer the grand, flashing lights of 'I Drove a Truck to Sierra Leone with No Fuel or Food and Saved 25,000 Grateful People'. We like sacrifice best when it is big, bouncy and happens once with a quick and noticeable amount of recognition. We're a tad slower to sign up for the long-term slog that accompanies the type of sacrifices that come our way more often.

I need to be careful with this next bit as I don't want to put anyone's name up in lights and turn their acts of sacrifice into fodder for cheap books. Still, there are a few people I know whose sacrifice has paid off, despite the fact that they felt ill-equipped to carry it through from the start. The church to which I belong (Soul Survivor Watford) has many faults, many of which have been conceived, nurtured and developed by me, the pastor. But in the summer of 1999, I was amazed; so many of the members gave themselves in all sorts of ways – small and not so small – to see that the Soul Survivor festivals ran smoothly. We put on three of them, back to back, and hosted over 16,000 people from around the world for almost three weeks. Sounds impressive? You should see the team; you couldn't imagine a more ordinary bunch. Yet they worked hard – often through the night – many giving up their holidays and sacrificing precious time just to be there to help other people get closer to their heavenly Father.

There was one time when those of us from the church who were down on site met up to chat and to pray. We were all tired and I watched the others shuffle in and settle down. One of the speakers was there to pray for and talk to us, and he came up with just the right words. 'You know,' he said, 'God's proud of you. He knows what you've given up and have sacrificed to put this on and he knows that as a church you have chosen to make this commitment.' Nearly everyone was quietly weeping and it suddenly hit me just what a sacrifice it was that they had made. You see, I love the festivals because I love showing off; I love being up on stage and seeing what God's doing around the place. But there would never have been any of the Soul Survivor festivals if it wasn't for an army of people quietly getting on with the dull, frustrating and downright difficult jobs that go on away from the public eye. It's like what Jesus said: 'When a grain of wheat falls into the ground and dies there is much fruit.' He was talking of himself, the grain that came to earth, died and in so doing produced the fruit of eternal life. I think he was also talking about something else. In the summer of 1999 I saw plenty of little grains of wheat, dying their own little deaths so that there might be plenty of fruit. Nearly 1,000 people became Christians that summer. None of it would have been possible if there weren't a group of struggling Christians from Soul Survivor Watford, getting tired, wet and fed up for the sake of people they had never met.

There's no limit to what God can do through a person who is totally dedicated to him. The one thing that God is looking for when he searches among his people are those who are willing to give up their lives for his sake and for that of the gospel. You know what? When we answer 'yes' to that question we find more life, joy and fulfilment than we could ever imagine.

I remember when I was leading the youth group at St Andrew's, Chorleywood. Among the number was an immaculately coiffured Matt Redman who, despite his obsession with combing and conditioning his hair, was developing an understanding of God's love of sacrifice. His school's drama department was very prestigious and he had been involved in productions for quite a while, doing increasingly well, even directing some of his friends in one particular production. One day we were travelling to a houseparty when he told me that he had decided to quit the boards and leave the drama behind. He said that God had told him he faced a choice, with the theatre on one side and worship on the other. 'Don't be ridiculous', came my spiritually enlightened reply. 'Of course you can carry on doing both.' Knowing that God had spoken to him and wanting to follow it through, Matt quit drama a while later. It proved to be an incredibly costly decision; not only did his friends not understand him but his teachers thought him a fool. He had to watch as productions came and went without him, something that was at times almost agonising. The point is that it was drama that he enjoyed the most – he came alive when he did it – but God had asked him whether he was prepared to lay it down for him.

There's a story in the Bible that takes the idea of sacrifice to a far greater level; God asks Abraham if he is prepared to give up the thing he values most, his son Isaac. It turns out that he is and he prepares to sacrifice him, literally. In the end God gave Isaac back to Abraham, but not before he had been ready to let him go. Matt never got drama back, except that in a strange way that I will never fully understand, out of that willingness to sacrifice came a blessing. These examples may be poles apart in terms of what was given up, but Matt was sure that God had told him to make his sacrifice, as was Abraham and as were the people who helped out at Soul Survivor 99. We might not be able to be confident that we can follow Jesus all the way along the road of sacrifice, but we can all start out with: 'Lord, I'd rather not do this, but it's not my will, but yours that I want to see done.' Out of that comes power; the sort that can change a world.

In our all-new consumer brand of Christianity

we're so keen to find the latest quick fix, the most shiny tool that will make us feel better. The power of the sacrificial life – the sort that Jesus taught us how to live – is the key to rising above this unchristian state and to move on to becoming the type of people who really will make a difference where it matters.

'Submit yourself to
death, death of your ambitions
and favourite wishes every day
and death of your whole body in
the end: submit every fibre
of your being, and you
will find eternal life.'
C.S. Lewis, *Mere Christianity*

'I look upon life
as a gift from God. I did nothing
to earn it. Now the time is coming
for me to give it back, I have
no right to complain.'
Joyce Cary

3

Dealing with Grief

So far in my life I've only had to face one major bereavement. About sixteen years ago my father had a heart attack. He managed to recover and for a while we all thought that he was getting better, but he soon seemed to get worse again. It never occurred to me at the time that this deterioration might signal the end, and I can remember being at work one day while my mother had gone to the hospital to pick him up after some tests. I got the phone call from her, the most horrendous phone call I've ever had. She told me to come to the hospital as the doctor had just told her that he had a week to live. Then she cried.

I can remember collecting my sister and rushing

to the hospital. That last week was terrible; we all knew that he was going and all that we could do was to watch him slip away. The night he died I sat next to him as his breathing got slower and slower. There were bigger and bigger gaps between breaths and my mind was racing. At about 3 a.m. there was one particular gap between breaths that was so drawn out that I stiffened, thinking that it was all over. Then he breathed again and I went back to waiting. I had held it all together until then – for days I hadn't cried or broken down – but that moment changed things and I started weeping. In the morning I was exhausted and my family told me to go home to get a little sleep. They stayed with him while I returned home.

As soon as the phone rang I knew what I was about to find out. I rushed back to the hospital to join the rest of my family in saying goodbye to the father and husband who had just died. It was the most bizarre feeling as we gathered round his bed, each giving him a kiss. The idea that that was it, he had gone and that we wouldn't see him again on this earth was the start of much more grief that was to follow. I'd find myself breaking down as I saw and experienced new things, reminded that he would never share any of them with me. It lasted a while. There were moments within the period of grief when it was easier, and there were moments (particularly for my mum) when it was much, much worse. I'll never forget the agony of the first Christmas without him. My sister's second child had just been born and the fact that he was not there, the fact that in our hands lay the beginnings of a life which he would never know and who would never know him, was almost too much to take.

All of us will go through periods of grief in our lives. We will all taste it – some sooner than others – and without exception we will all encounter different levels of it as we experience the passing of those close and others not so close to us. We are all going to lose a loved one – that much we know for sure – but how should we (as Christians) deal with it? What help can we find from the Bible and what we know of God that can be of assistance as we work our way through?

Losing my father brought about a big change in the way I felt about things as a Christian. Previously I had thought about death and grief in strict theological terms. I knew the theory and I applied it to my conscious mind deliberately and with some degree of precision. Once I had collided head on with the agony of grief, all that theological rhetoric went out of the window and left me not so much thinking about things but feeling them in the most intense way imaginable. I was ruled by the emotions and pleaded with

God for an answer to the biggest question that we can ask; why?

The truth is that just in the same way that my questions came from the guts, bypassing logic, so too does God's answer make little sense to our minds. It is something that exists beyond the limits of our limited rational thinking. We cannot place God in a box and we cannot explain with words many of the things he does. Accepting death at any time is bound to be hard, but when it involves someone who has been taken way before their time, working through the grief can almost seem impossible. Where is logic for the mother who mourns her teenage daughter knocked down by a drunk driver? Where is rational argument for the partner who mourns the loss of their loved one, left alone to bring up a family?

So we cannot reduce grief to a set of rules and regulations, giving directions, reasons and arguments to ensure that all come out of it unscathed. Grief is emotional, it is important, and we do ourselves wrong if we try to bottle it up, ignore it or pretend that we can get by without it.

But just as we spent the last chapter looking at the way that life is made up of little deaths, of sacrifices that mark our Christian path, so too it is made up of little griefs. Grief is not just limited to the death of a loved one; we all go through a similar process of mourning at many other points in our lives, often ones quite separate from actual physical death. For example, realising that a relationship is over, that an ambition may never be fulfilled or that a hope is empty, all these will take us through a grieving process. Through it we will begin to reconstruct our lives around the gap of something we had always assumed was – or would eventually be – there.

One of the first things that happens when we grieve is to face disbelief. It's common for people to deny the death of a person soon after it has happened. Just the other day I was getting towed back from Wales listening to the AA man tell me about some of the experiences he had collected in over twenty-one years of service. He told me about one time that he had been called out by the police to attend to a car with a broken windscreen. It had broken when the driver had knocked down a child one hundred yards down the road. Despite the fact that the man had just killed this child, the AA guy told me how the driver was talking away as if nothing had happened, making jokes and small talk all the way to the garage. There was something almost sickening about the story, as if the man was going too far in his denial, and the AA man never found out what happened to him later.

I'm sure that it came home in a big way but, nevertheless, even if it isn't quite so dramatic for us, it's not unusual to find that the reality of death takes a while to sink in.

When I realised that no one was going to wave a magic wand and stop the inevitable from happening to my father, as I waited between his breathing in and breathing out in the middle of the night, the tears came. I didn't want to do it, but something told me that I had to begin to believe that this was the end. As the days followed the struggle between denial and acceptance carried on, not so much as an all-out war that was over at any specific point, but as a series of battles and skirmishes as I realised that he would no longer be around in a whole variety of different scenarios.

In many ways this picture of grief as a series of random events rather than set stages is one that I find helpful. I think it's highly unlikely that any two people's experiences of grief will be absolutely identical. So we need to be easy on ourselves and others, finding the balance between allowing the process to follow its own path and pace, and encouraging a general movement through the stages we're outlining here.

One of the things that many people find they experience during a grieving process is anger. Sometimes the anger can be directed at God himself as questions are fired at him in the midst of the confusion. How could he let that person die? How could he let that dream fall through? How could he let that relationship break up? Often we can spend some time in this stage, something which can in itself cause us to feel guilty about harbouring such thoughts and resentments towards God.

Through the film *Shadowlands* many of us have found out more about C.S. Lewis's life. He married late and had a wonderful marriage to Joy, who contracted cancer and died long before 'her time'. He wrote about his feelings after her death in a little book called *A Grief Observed* (Faber, 1961). There's one paragraph that stands out from the rest:

Not that I am, I think, in much danger of ceasing to believe in God. The real danger is to coming to believe such dreadful things about him. The conclusion I dread is not 'so there's no God after all' but 'this is what God is really like; deceive yourself no longer'.

That seems to echo something that I and many others have been through: a period of despair. I've known people who, because of some tragedy in their lives, have tried to say 'there is no God' and question how he could exist in the face of such cruelty. After the First World War there was a significant drop in belief in God throughout Britain which many put down to the horrors witnessed on the battlefields and the grief of those at home. The trenches at Flanders sent people back with the question, 'How can there be a God if this can happen?' I've known other people who have kept up their belief but have doubted his character, just as C.S. Lewis feared.

On the other side there are those who are aware of these two possibilities, and who try to avoid them by denying the existence of any such feelings at all. Call it what you want – stiff upper lip or religious repression – there are plenty who have struggled bravely on, accepting death but denying that grief has any part in their own lives. Of course a desire to hold on to God is to be applauded, but in fact this repression can often cause far more long-term harm than good.

It's also completely unbiblical. I love to read the psalms; they are raw emotion. The psalmist appears to be totally at ease with the extremes of his heart. Not only is he able to praise God for his infinite goodness, but he is able to express the darker side of things. 'Where are you?' he asks. 'I weep on my bed all night . . . my enemies have me surrounded . . . you've deserted me.' It seems to me that he has permission to pray prayers that are so close to the edge that they almost appear to be blasphemous. He has permission to express the doubt, the horror and the pain, just as we do. Through the honest expression of such difficult feelings we – like David – end up at peace with God. First there's the denial, then the anger and the despair, and finally there comes the restoration of peace.

On the other side of grief is a wonderful thing called acceptance. Not only do we find that we can accept things as they are, but we can feel accepted by God, that he both understands and shares our feelings, from the beginning to the end. C.S. Lewis finally knew that God was with him throughout the time he mourned the death of his wife, despite the fact that for much of the time Lewis was not aware of God. Even when his desperation was so great that without realising it he pushed God away, God was still there, with him, sharing his grief.

As I've said we can grieve over all sorts of things, but before we get too analytical about things, we need to get back to basics. We need to learn to express our grief, to give it a voice and allow it to be heard. Nothing is too bad to be brought before God; no despair or anger is too much to be laid before him. If we don't express it, we bury it. Once buried it can eat away at us, decaying the good that once was there.

We come back to the cross once again. After

all, who better to let it all out on than Almighty God – the one who gave up most, who sacrificed more than anyone else? Jesus shares in the experience of humanity on a level that we will never understand when he says, 'My God, my God, why have you forsaken me?' The words can be such a comfort to us as they are proof positive of the fact that he has been there, to the darkest place. Jesus has been there ahead of us, separated from God where things simply don't get any worse.

When things go wrong each of us faces a choice. It might seem like bad timing, but this choice is a vitally important one. It proves the maturity of our relationship with God. Either we turn from him and get bitter or we turn to him, express the pain, call out to him and get better. Either we can be like the little child who will not receive comfort but who keeps running away in floods of tears, or we can be like the child who cries and cries in its parent's arms. Sometimes we may need to do a little wriggling, sometimes we may need to punch out, but the arms of a parent are strong, strong enough to take the blows.

Coming to the end of grief also brings us face to face with a choice. As Christians we all face the option of whether or not we will trust God and all his goodness. With the psalmist we can paint it as black as we really see it and still find it in us to wind up saying, 'Yet will I rejoice and trust in you.' We can be honest about the circumstances much as Habakkuk was:

> Though the fig-tree does not bud
>   and there are no grapes on the vines,
> though the olive crop fails
>   and the fields produce no food,
> though there are no sheep in the pen
>   and no cattle in the stalls,
> yet I will rejoice in the Lord,
>   I will be joyful in God my saviour.
> (Habakkuk 3:17–18)

Basically, Habby got to the place where even if everything went wrong – even something totally disastrous like the olive crop failing – he wouldn't let his own pain and anxiety get in the way of his faith in God. But crucially, he didn't fall into the trap of pretending that the pain was not there.

Choosing to put our faith in God is itself a healing act, and we emerge the other side with a strengthened faith and a relationship one step closer towards maturity. This reminds me of the story of the disciples in the boat as Jesus walked towards them one stormy night on the Sea of Galilee. They were all afraid, yet Peter sussed that it might be the

Lord. 'If that's you,' he said 'just show me that it's you and I'll come.' We can walk on the water, through the storms of life, when we know that it's Jesus in front of us and him we are heading towards. What I take from this story when looked at in the context of grief is that when there are storms all around us, when the waves look too big and the grief and pain threaten to overpower us, there is just one question that matters: will we follow Jesus? When we hear his voice, will we be brave enough to step out from the fragile security constructed around us and make ourselves even more vulnerable by trusting Jesus and turning towards him? We're very fond of overcomplicating our faith, yet it really is that simple, and – depending on how the storms of life are treating you at the moment – it really is that easy/hard.

Having said that we need to be honest as we move through the grieving process, there also comes a place where an expression of trust in God acts as praise, even in the midst of pain. Some of the most amazing times of worship that we can have on earth this side of heaven are the times when we worship when it hurts, when it's a sacrifice. It happened to King David, who mourned the death of the son born out of his extramarital affair with Bathsheba. As soon as he heard that the child had died he washed his face and went to rejoice and praise his heavenly Father, the one who had forgiven him so much.

There is an aspect of that determination which we can see in Paul's letter to the Philippians. Even though he was writing from a jail and circumstances really could not have been worse, he wrote a letter about rejoicing in the Lord. We know that on one particular occasion while in jail he was having such a storming late-night worship session that the very doors that kept him captive flew open.

But we need to be careful. This is not about using worship as a means of escape from reality – the Christian faith is certainly not an escapist one – but there is a rejoicing that comes in the acknowledgement of the fact that life hurts yet praise can still take place. This is not because we're defective or bottling things up; it is because God is good. Not only does he deserve a sacrifice of praise – the sort that costs something, that takes place even when we don't particularly feel like it – but worship of him is also infinitely compatible with our pain. As we have seen, he's been through it all already.

Romans 8:28 brings us a truth that: 'we know that in all things God works for the good of those who love him, who have been called according to his purposes.' There is a very real sense that some of the things that we cannot see this side of heaven cannot be understood. All we see is the pain and the grief, yet from heaven's perspective there is an answer, there is a bigger picture into which all these things fit. To rejoice is to trust heaven's perspective. Believing in that bigger picture and the absolute goodness of the artist behind it requires nothing less than a leap of faith.

'All who have faith
in Jesus Christ can know the
strength of his presence, helping
them to deal with grief and, when
the time comes, to face
death itself.'

Harold Bauman, *Living Through Grief*

'Until our Master summons
us, not a hair on our head can
perish, not a moment of our life
can be snatched away from us.
When he sends for us, it should
seem but the message that the
child is wanted at home.'

Anthony Thorold

4

The Second Coming

In a book this size I have decided not to look at the issues surrounding Jesus' return, such as will he come before the earth goes through a tribulation which will last a thousand years, or will he return after? What are the signs we should look for? Some of these questions have kept Christian theologians arguing happily for years as to what the Bible actually says. The purpose of this chapter is limited to unpacking the consequences of the wonderful truth that he will return!

This book has been oozing its way out of my subconscious as the calendar has rolled from 1999 into 2000. So far Millennium Night Fever appears to have been rather a lot of fuss about nothing, and right now people around the world are busy trying to justify the US$328 billion spent on 'fixing' the Y2K bug. While the prophecies of planes falling out of the sky and toasters refusing to co-operate seem to have been a little over the top, the cause for millennial madness wasn't only restricted to computers. As expected there were a few people predicting the return of Jesus, and security was tight around Jerusalem and other key sites in the Holy Land. There were fears that wacky Christians would carry out threats to do their bit for revival by planting bombs, but again, everything seemed to pass smoothly.

While the trees and tinsel have gone, I'm still left thinking about things; it wasn't just the nutters who thought about Armageddon. I spoke to plenty of friends about this over the period, and many of them were surprised to admit that they too had ended up thinking about things eternal. So what was it that made so many of us turn our minds – however briefly – to the subject of the Second Coming? What makes me so sure that I would recognise it if it did come in my lifetime? Am I thinking about it because I'm bored or can I really be so arrogant to believe that Jesus would choose my time over any other to pay up on his promise and come back for his people?

Why should we even bother considering the Second Coming? Isn't it best left to those with a passion for home-made explosives and a gift for losing the plot? I hope not, and I'm sure that to do so would be to throw the baby out with the bath water. Whenever I start to feel confused about things I generally try and remind myself of the importance of looking back as well as looking forward. After all, it seemed to work for the Israelites; every so often they would stop and go over all the good things that God had done. In reminding themselves of their history and unique relationship with God, they would get all fired up about their future. Viewed in context of God's always being there and being continually gracious and mighty to save, it's not surprising that God's people after Jesus' life on earth have looked forward to his return.

Part of my confusion comes from the fact that the Second Coming is one of those subjects that hasn't been talked about in the Church much over the last couple of decades. We might have dusted it off at a couple of points in the calendar, but in general the return of Christ has been left on the unpreached sermon pile, somewhere between homosexuality and Leviticus. I think that's a shame. Of course we don't want to end up being too heavenly minded to be any earthly good, but I firmly believe that there is a whole stack of lessons waiting to be learnt from taking a good hard look at the return of our Lord Jesus Christ.

When I was a frighteningly fresh Christian I was keen. I was also intensely sensitive, slow to think things through for myself and prone to getting scared easily. Together these character traits led me into a head-on collision with the most disturbing film I have ever seen. As part of the RE curriculum the teacher decided to do a little evangelism on the sly and make some fresh recruits for the cause by scaring them senseless. He chose to show a film called *A Thief in the Night* – a dramatic representation of the Second Coming as depicted in the Bible. Along with a few of my mates who had also become Christians a month before, I watched as the film played out. With some seriously awful 1970s photography and some acting the likes of which are usually reserved for public information films on the dangers of leaving the gas on, the film worked its way through a number of scenes. A regular family were sat at home when all of a sudden two were taken away and three were left. A group were walking along the road one minute, and one of them had vanished the next. The film went on to show other aspects of what might happen when Jesus returns, and as it finished the whole class sat in a stunned silence. A friend of mine refused to sleep for almost three nights, choosing instead to be like one of the wise virgins and stare out of his bedroom window in case Jesus made a sneak return to Harrow in the wee small hours. I managed to spend almost a year avoiding fields and cosy family situations where the total number of those present equalled five.

Despite the fact that many of us acted a little strangely after the film, looking back now I'm convinced that it did us some good in the long term. Not only did it get us excited about a central truth of Christianity – that Jesus will return – but it also got us into reading our Bibles in a way that we hadn't quite done before.

Perhaps a film like *A Thief in the Night* would not get made today precisely because of the new millennium. During the years sandwiching the start of the twenty-first century it has almost become a bit of a cliché to talk about things of an apocalyptic nature. After all, everyone knows that there are plenty of nutters out there preaching hellfire and impending destruction, why give the rest of the population the satisfaction of playing up to the stereotype? Yet I think we can go too far in shying away from the subject. Perhaps we need to have restored to us a sense of biblical balance about the whole thing.

OK, so we might have sussed that this whole Second Coming thing is worth the chat, but that brings us neatly on to the next confusing issue: what will it look like? The New Testament church had a far better hold on this than we do. They managed to believe passionately in Jesus' promise and allow it to fire them up to live radical lives at the same time as managing not to appear like dribbling loonies. Quite an achievement.

Acts 1 shows them all hanging around as Jesus returns to heaven. He tells them to hold back in Jerusalem where they are to wait for his Holy Spirit to introduce himself and fill them up.

> After he said this, he was taken up before their very eyes, and a cloud hid him from their sight. They were looking intently up into the sky as he was going, when suddenly two men dressed in white stood beside them. 'Men of Galilee,' they said, 'why do you stand there looking into the sky? This same Jesus, who has been taken from you into heaven, will come back in the same way you have seen him go into heaven.'
>
> (Acts 1:9–11)

Do you get that? Jesus is coming back in the same way he returned to heaven. It's astounding stuff, but we miss the point if we don't pay proper attention. Jesus may have left on the clouds, but his first arrival was very different. He came to earth – God made flesh – as a baby. He was both impoverished and unrecognised – to many people he would even have been unremarkable. Only if you were in the know would you have had a clue about the future that lay in front of him. But the Second Coming won't be marked by secrecy or stealth; as the angels said, Jesus will come again in the clouds. This time there will be no doubt about whether he really has arrived or not, and his return will be accompanied by him bringing justice and the rule of heaven in all its fullness. As with those in the early church, we too are living in the in-between times, straddling time from the point that Jesus left the earth to the moment of his return. His final trip will be to end the established order and bring about a new heaven and a new earth.

Then I saw a new heaven and a new earth, for the first heaven and the first earth had passed away, and there was no longer any sea. I saw the Holy City, the new Jerusalem, coming down out of heaven from God, prepared as the bride beautifully dressed for her husband. And I heard a loud voice from the throne saying, 'Now the dwelling of God is with men, and he will live with them. They will be his people, and God himself will be with them and be their God. He will wipe every tear from their eyes. There will be no more death or mourning or crying or pain, for the old order of things has passed away.'

(Revelation 21:1–4)

We know from Scripture that Jesus will return to look for the Church – his bride – whom he expects to find waiting for him. His longing is that we will be looking forward to his arrival, and for that reason

I'm convinced that we need to spend more time looking into every aspect of the Second Coming.

The fact that Jesus is returning has certain implications for us. What exactly does it mean when the Bible says that he will bring his rule, authority and justice completely to us? Yes, we may have a taste of it already – we may think we know a little of his kingdom and the ways things should be – but do we really know what it will look like in the flesh? True, the kingdom of God is here in part, but it is incomplete. 'Creation,' as Paul writes in Romans 8:19, 'waits in eager expectation for the sons of God to be revealed.' The phrase 'creation waits' can easily be translated as 'creation groans'. I believe that part of this groaning is the waiting for the story to be completed, for the prophecies to be fulfilled.

The Bible tells us that eventually we will receive our resurrection bodies – the Mike Pilavachi I was created to be – and we will live on the new earth – the planet as God intended, free from pollution, corruption and the effects of hatred. We won't be going to Mars and turning left; the new earth will be very much right here.

The presence of justice as a key factor in the Second Coming brings us on to the slightly less attractive subject of judgement. While many of us might prefer it if we all could go on happily ever after regardless of how we lived our lives, it is impossible to separate justice from judgement. When the Lord returns he will be angrier than any of us could ever imagine. Before you start contemplating a career change to Buddhism, don't forget that our interpretations of anger should not be confused with God's. His isn't an indiscriminate, broken-bottle-in-hand type of rage, unfairly mowing down all who dare to cross his path. His is a righteous anger, putting things back the way they should be; those who have done wrong receiving what they deserve. Don't we hate it when crimes go unpunished? God's judgement is the best there is, and unlike many of the poor imitations we see on earth, it is something to be looked forward to.

So then, what about hell? As the point of heaven is not so much about angels, harps and clouds as it is about eternal relationship with God, so the point of hell is not about the fire, brimstone and lakes of sulphur. Hell is eternal separation from God. If someone who has heard the gospel in this life but has died rejecting Jesus – and therefore rejecting relationship with God as Father – then the Bible makes clear that their choice lasts for ever. That's hard on the person concerned, but we need to remember that it's even harder on God. It's the sort of pain any parent would feel as their kid walks out on them, wanting no more to do with them. So what about babies who die before they've had a chance to hear about Jesus? Surely it isn't fair for them to be hell-bound too? The Bible doesn't make itself incredibly clear on this point, except that we are told to trust in God's mercy, grace and love. I don't think that for a moment a baby in this situation would go to hell. This is a tough subject, perhaps even the toughest. It's good for us to realise though, that the choices we human beings make now have eternal consequences. We all deserve eternal separation from God because of our sin. The cross is God's way of bridging the gap. Jesus did the horrendous bit by dying for us; all we have to do is come to the cross. Is that really such a bad deal?

I find Peter's second letter to the Church at large to be essential reading when it comes to the end of time. He takes the reader through some fairly fundamental stuff, spelling it out clearly.

First of all, you must understand that in the last days scoffers will come, scoffing and following their own evil desires. They will say, 'Where is this "coming" he promised? Ever since our fathers died, everything goes on as it has since the beginning of creation.' But they deliberately forget that long ago by God's word the heavens existed and the earth was formed out of water and by water. By these waters also the world of that time was deluged and destroyed. By the same word the present heavens and earth are reserved for fire, being kept for the day of judgment and destruction of ungodly men. But do not forget this one thing, dear friends: With the Lord a day is like a thousand years and a thousand years are like a day.

(2 Peter 3:3–8)

When it comes to God, time is relative. Just because we have a few scoffers doing their scoffing thing around us, just because theories of evolution may appear to some to rule out God's hand, we must never forget that God's timing is not ours. 'The Lord is not slow in keeping his promise, as some understand slowness. He is patient with you, not wanting anyone to perish, but everyone to come to repentance' (2 Peter 3:9).

So here we have it; the core of this issue of God's timing. We might be thinking that 2,000 years is pushing it as far as waiting for Jesus' return might be – we share those confusions and frustrations with the people around Peter who had waited just thirty-seven years since Jesus returned to heaven. The delay is easily explained; God wants everyone to be saved and in relationship with him before he returns in judgement. His 'slowness' is only there because of his goodness. In a sense, the more years that pass without his return, the more reason we have to praise and worship him as he holds back from final judgement for the sake of those who might not make it through.

> But the day of the Lord will come like a thief. The heavens will disappear with a roar; the elements will be destroyed by fire, and the earth and everything in it will be laid bare. Since everything will be destroyed in this way, what kind of people ought you to be? You ought to live holy and godly lives as you look forward to the day of God and speed its coming.
>
> (2 Peter 3:10–12)

And here is the key: why should we be looking forward to the Second Coming of Jesus? Because when we have him as our focus and our hope, when we understand that one day he will return in bodily form, we will live the type of lives that reflect his nature, and in doing so quicken his return. The Church is called the bride of Christ in the Bible, and one day when Jesus returns there is going to be the mother of all weddings. As people who love him, we can look forward to his return in hope, not in anxiety.

> That day will bring about the destruction of the heavens by fire, and the elements will melt in the heat. But in keeping with his promise we are looking forward to a new heaven and a new

earth, the home of righteousness. So then, dear friends, since you are looking forward to this, make every effort to be found spotless, blameless and at peace with him.

(2 Peter 3:12–14)

The Second Coming is definitely bad news for certain people. For those who have lived selfish and self-centred lives, for those who have been greedy, immoral and who have made themselves comfortable and rich at the expense of the poor, and who have completely rejected him, the return of Jesus will not be something to celebrate, to put it mildly. But for the Church, it's what we're living for.

But hey, guys, let's not get smug about it. The knowledge of Jesus' return should spur us on to tell as many people about him as possible in the meantime. Just as the first Christians – who expected Jesus' return at any time – were urgent in their evangelism, so should we be.

'Eternal life is a
gift from God, and the key that
releases it to us is faith.'
David Winter, *What Happens after Death*

5

How to Die a Good Death

My friend Matt Redman has a younger brother named Thomas. I've known him and the rest of the family for years and have seen them all go through various phases as they have grown up. One phase that Thomas would probably rather forget is his Flopsy-the-Bunny stage. He was ten and decided to get himself a rabbit. He and his mother made a hutch and a run in the garden and Thomas went out and bought Flopsy, a large white thing with – you may have guessed – floppy ears. Days came and went and all Thomas ever seemed keen to talk about was Flopsy; the reports came almost hourly and I counted it a splendid privilege to know exactly how many bites of her carrot the dear thing had taken at any specific time.

A few weeks after Flopsy's arrival I dropped by unannounced to catch up on the latest instalment of 'Flopsy Eats a Cucumber', when I was greeted at the door by the entire family, ashen-faced and deadly quiet. I came in and joined them in staring across the hall, where I could see Flopsy lying on a radiator. I count myself an expert in neither rabbits nor death, but I could tell that something was most definitely wrong. My question about whether the rabbit was dead was met by denials and murmurings about how Flopsy wasn't dead, she was simply cold and needed a little warming up. None of them wanted to admit the truth and for a while I too joined them in telling myself that just a few more minutes on the scorching radiator would bring her back to life. It didn't last and after a while I could stand it no more.

'I think she's dead, guys,' I said.

Thomas burst into tears. I felt awful and wished I was wrong, but it was no use. Flopsy was a gonner and slowly the rest of the family began to come round to the idea. Somehow I ended up with the job of burying the rabbit in the back garden. Now, I'm about as good at gardening as I am at figure skating, so when I saw how frosty and frozen over the ground was, I began to panic. After what seemed like hours of digging I admitted defeat and announced that the grave would simply have to do, unconventional as it was. Where most graves are long and thin, allowing the body to be laid horizontally, Flopsy's final resting place was deep and narrow, requiring her to be buried vertically. After a considerable struggle I managed to get her in – using a technique approximately the opposite to removing a cork from a bottle with a corkscrew – and sat back to admire my handiwork. Thomas looked on aghast from his bedroom window.

The whole episode made me think about how keen we all are to skirt around the subject of death, regarding it as a wholly bad thing. But is that really the truth? Are we destined to be dragged kicking and screaming towards an undignified and horrendous ending of our days on earth? I don't really know anyone who I would say has had a particularly good death – at least I haven't seen any first hand – but reading the account of Jesus' death as told in the New Testament, I'm convinced that death has plenty of potential. Jesus' death was a lot more than just simply 'good'; it was brilliant.

In November 1999 I had some pains in my chest and stomach. Instead of being the usual side effects of one late-night curry too many, these seemed sharper and altogether more intense. Of course I thought I was dying – I usually do whenever I'm bored and slightly ill – but this time my convictions that I was about to meet my maker were altogether more real. Instead of being the usual call for attention and entertainment, I actually felt as though

I was telling the truth. I was shocked; usually I use the 'I think I'm dying' as a way of passing the time and whipping up a little extra sympathy or a free dinner. It never stops me from carrying on my daily routine. This time things were different; the pains got worse and were refusing to go away, and it looked as though I was even going to have to cancel a fast-approaching trip to Holland. The day before we were due to leave I finally gave in and blew the trip out, retiring to lie curled up beneath my dining-room table, moaning quietly to myself. This had me worried, because usually I would choose a far more public place (like the office) in which to do my moaning.

Soon afterwards some friends came round to check up on me. They took one look and called the doctor who asked to have my symptoms described to him over the phone in greater detail. His response didn't exactly do my confidence much good as he suggested that an ambulance be phoned immediately as he suspected a heart attack.

It wasn't a heart attack, in case you're wondering. It was something far less glamorous (gall stones), but for a moment I can honestly say that I thought my time was up. Waiting for the ambulance, wondering whether the heart attack was about to kick in for real and finish me off, I went through a bizarre selection of thoughts. As well as worrying about who was going to pick up my shoes from the menders, my mind was filled with the sense that I couldn't die just yet as there was so much more that I wanted to do. I'm sure most of us would feel something similar.

For Jesus it was different. Sure he died young – younger than me when I thought I was on my way out – but it's clear from the Bible that there was not one ounce of regret, not a hint of remorse that time had been wasted or that there was still more to be done. Jesus' whole life was a lead up to his death. When he came to earth he began a journey that didn't end, but that culminated in the cross. Death was not a cruel and early stop to a match in progress; it was the perfect goal after the perfect build-up that won the match. We see that Jesus' life was a preparation for his death, and his death was a vital part of his coming to earth. In Jesus' case, death and life were perfect partners, each one dependent on the other, combining to alter the course of history for ever.

As Christians, Jesus' death should make us look at death in a very different way. Instead of murmuring under the table we should recognise that through the cross we have a power that blows death out of the water. 'Death, thou shalt die', wrote John Donne, and he was right. In a one-on-one fight Jesus kicked death's butt royally. There simply isn't a contest any more and through Jesus – his mighty power and glorious resurrection – we have nothing to fear.

For me, the very core of Jesus' death being a good one is that he actually chose it. He was prepared for it and knew that he was dying for a purpose; to bring us life and allow us to know God. As he was dying on the cross, Jesus made seven statements that I'm convinced are the most incredible statements that a person could make as they are dying. While it's not precisely clear from the Bible which order they were said in – different Gospels give you different versions – I've put them in an order that makes sense to me. What is clear though, is that these are words which will live for ever.

In Luke 23:34 Jesus says, 'Father, forgive them, for they do not know what they are doing.' What had they done? Together with the occupying Roman forces, his fellow Jews had falsely accused him, lied about him, beaten, tormented and tortured him. He could have rained down fire on them, poured out a string of verbal abuse and threats or called down all manner of curses upon them. Instead he forgave them, making sure that the Jesus we see on the cross acts 100 per cent in line with the Jesus that we have read about beforehand.

His death on the cross becomes even more amazing when we realise exactly who the 'they' were that Jesus was referring to when he asked his

Father to grant forgiveness. It wasn't just the authorities or the soldiers that Jesus was talking about, it was us. Jesus' death was caused by us; we sent him there. My sin and yours were the ticket that led him to the place where he paid for all our sin. Make no mistake, when it comes to our wrongdoing and habit of living our lives away from God, there was only one true sacrifice that could have been made to secure our relationship with him. As a just God, our heavenly Father could not let our sin pass without a just punishment, and Jesus paid the price on our behalf when he took our place on the cross.

In his holiness God judged that the payback for sin is death, but in his love he also decided that he would send the most precious thing that he had to pay the price so that he might have us back. Jesus, as he hung on the cross, said through the pain and the agony, 'Father, forgive Mike Pilavachi as he doesn't know what he is doing.'

Moving to Mark's version of the life of Jesus we come across these words in chapter 15 verse 34: 'My God, my God, why have you forsaken me?' To understand the true horror of these words it is vital that we understand how for eternity, God the Son and God the Father were continually united. For the time that he hung on the cross God the Son knew the agony of separation from his Father. It was a key part of the punishment for sin that simply could not be avoided.

Sadly, the idea of being separated from God for a time probably does not fill us with the same sense of fear and dread as it did Jesus. But for many of us, as we die our little deaths or agonise over the death of a loved one, this sense of loss is a vaguely familiar taste to our lips. When things go wrong in our lives we can often feel something of what Jesus felt, as though God is a million miles away and nothing can seem to bring him back. Jesus not only shared but felt more deeply than we could ever feel that sense of forsakenness.

Third, in John 19:26–7 we read that Jesus sees John the apostle and Mary his mother standing together around the cross, watching him die. Can you imagine what it must have been like for Jesus' own mother to watch her firstborn son die on the cross, crucified like a common criminal? Jesus says to his mother: 'Dear woman, here is your son.' And to John: 'Here is your mother.'

What is he saying here? He brings home the message that his death makes us family. Because he died we not only have reconciliation with God the Father, but we can also have reconciliation as a human race. In fact, that is precisely what the Church is supposed to be; the family of Jesus here on earth.

All this might read very well on paper, but you may be wondering whether it actually works out there in reality. I can honestly say that I've seen people – and I'm thinking of two in particular – who have hated each other with such passion and bitterness that the prospect of any form of forgiveness passing between them has been about as remote as remote can be. Having met with Jesus and understood what he did for them on the cross they have been filled with the power to be reconciled to each other. Amazing.

John 19:28 shows that at one point Jesus cried out, 'I am thirsty.' Once he did that the guards offered him a sponge dipped in vinegar, a cruel act as there was no way that such a drink would quench his thirst. But Jesus' thirst was not limited only to the physical; it was as if he wanted more of God. The thirst that was in Jesus, his desire to return home, went hand in hand with a knowledge that it was God and God alone who could satisfy him. And so we have a picture of Jesus on the cross, alone and separated from his Father yet still holding on to the fact that he is utterly dependent on him for sustenance and support.

The next saying can be found in Luke 23:42–3. Luke tells us that Jesus was crucified in between two criminals, possibly thieves. One of them joined in the mocking of Jesus, challenging him to save himself if he really was who he said he was. The other quietened him down and pointed out that while the two of them deserved what they were getting, Jesus had done nothing whatsoever to warrant crucifixion.

> Then he said, 'Jesus, remember me when you come into your kingdom.'
> Jesus answered him, 'I tell you the truth, today you will be with me in paradise.'

And that was the reason that Jesus came: to save repentant criminals like the thief, like me and like you. 'Today you will be with me in paradise' is the word of hope that not only would have turned that man's life upside down, but which can alter the course of our lives for ever. For all of us who ask his forgiveness Jesus' reply is the same.

This takes us back to another thing that Jesus said long before he died, this time reported in John 14:1–3:

> Do not let your hearts be troubled. Trust in God; trust also in me. In my Father's house are many rooms; if it were not so, I would have told you. I am going there to prepare a place for you. And if I go and prepare a place for you, I will come back and take you to be with me so that you also may be where I am.

Jesus' earlier encouragement for us not to focus on death as an ultimate end but as a gateway between now and something wonderful should not be forgotten. The profound truth that he has even gone on ahead to prepare things for us is enough to blow my mind.

Sometimes I wonder what heaven will be like; boring, perhaps. Endless angels twanging their flippin' harps as eternity whiles itself away in some kind of easy-listening pastiche. I hope not. If Jesus is preparing a place for me, that means it is a place that will fit me. I don't mean physically, but spiritually I know that I shall be at peace, that I will have come home to a paradise of all-embracing love.

The sixth saying of Jesus on the cross can be found in John 19:30, made up of three simple words: 'It is finished.' Jesus came to suffer for us, to pay a price and settle the issue of our approach to God once and for ever. Moments before death he knew that the job was complete and that we had been bought back with his life.

Lastly, Luke 23:46 gives us the final words he uttered on the cross: 'Father, into your hands I commit my spirit.' I'd like to think that I could, but I'm not sure that I would have either the grace or the certainty to be able to mark the end of my life with any sort of comment about how sure I was of my place with God. For Jesus it was different; not only did he know that he had done enough, but he also trusted his Father at what is for most people the most terrifying moment of their lives. The amazing thing for us as Christians is that even with death staring us in our face, we can trust our heavenly Father, we can be sure that his goodness and power will win out, even beyond the grave.

'Death — the last sleep?
No, it's the final awakening.'
Walter Scott

'What the caterpillar calls
the end of the world, the master
calls a butterfly.'
Richard Bach

'If man hasn't discovered
something that he will die for,
he isn't fit to live.'
Martin Luther King

'The valley of the
shadow of death holds no
darkness for the child of God.
There must be light, else there
would be no shadow. Jesus is the
light. He has overcome death.'
Dwight L. Moody

6

Heaven, Angels
and All That

I've heard it said – in fact, I've even written it myself – that some people are too heavenly minded to be of any earthly use. This critique usually gets levelled at people fond of ranting about doomsday on street corners or suggesting that behind every nasty cough or piece of criticism is an army of demons. Like all soundbites it has a pleasant ring to it and acts as a brilliant put-down in defence of the type of Christian who tries to break free of the 'nutty Christian' label. But there's a problem with it, one that betrays our severe lack of understanding about heaven, angels and all that. You see, I don't think that heaven is all white clouds, fairies and harps. I think it's real, practical, passionate, relevant and good. To be truly heavenly-minded is not something I think we should be ashamed of; instead it is to catch hold of the pulse that courses through God's veins (if he has veins), to be in tune with his heart. God is no tweed-wearing-elbow-patched-grandpa, scared of us humans and unable to comprehend what makes us tick. Let's not forget that it is us who are made in *his* image, us who carry some of his genes. If anything is going to be of use on this earth it's getting suitably topped up with a continual dose of heavenly-mindedness, catching hold of God's thoughts, passions and plans. Let's not do heaven the disservice of assuming that it's all flowing robes and no substance; instead it might be of help if we could find out a little more about exactly what it is like.

To have a vision of heaven and a clearer picture of what the future holds is the best form of equipment we could ask for to serve God in this life. It's no coincidence that some of the people who have had the surest knowledge of how things are going to work out for us have gone on to serve God in the most wonderful of ways. It simply is not true that we can get away with putting up our feet and taking it easy while on earth, brushing aside the question of heaven and eternity with the flimsy argument that it can all be dealt with once we've moved on to that next level. *Wrong!* Eternal life starts now; as soon as you've been granted a glimpse of it, as soon as you've hooked up with Jesus then heaven is an active concern in your life.

When Jesus came to earth for the first time, it seemed that everybody was expecting him to turn up with the kingdom of God in tow. They thought that his arrival would mark the beginnings of heaven on earth, ending poverty, misery and all forms of oppression. In a way they were right; the kingdom did come, but not in all its fullness. We might see parts of the kingdom of God – his rule and authority – scattered here and there, but the day will come when we see it break out across the whole earth in all its life-changing fullness.

We often seem to struggle to comprehend the eternal. We get hung up on the fact that we cannot seem to understand the invisible nature of God. The temptation to sign up to the forces of materialism – as well as giving fuel to the injustice of poverty – can lead us even further down the path of 'if I can see it, I'll believe it'. We learn how to rely on the physical rather than the spiritual.

There's a great story in 2 Kings 6 where Elisha and his servant are surrounded by a tribe named the Aramaens. There are far more of these Aramaens than there are Israelites, and verse 15 brings us to the verge of battle:

When the servant of the man of God [Elisha] got up and went out early the next morning, an army with horses and chariots had surrounded the city. 'Oh, my lord, what shall we do?' the servant asked.

'Don't be afraid,' the prophet answered. 'Those who are with us are more than those who are with them.'

And Elisha prayed, 'O Lord, open his eyes so that he may see.' Then the Lord opened the servant's eyes, and he looked and saw the hills full of horses and chariots of fire all around Elisha.

(2 Kings 6:15–17)

After that the enemy came to attack Elisha and the rest of his crew and, due to some sneaky manoeuvres, the enemy wound up well and truly beaten. So often our problem is that – like Elisha's servant – we only see the physical problems. We get bogged down with details of money, people or circumstance. Instead we need to echo Elisha's prayer, asking the Lord to open our eyes so that we too can see that 'those who are with us are more than those who are against us'. As wacky and as thoroughly unpostmodern as it may sound, there is a spiritual world, a realm invisible to us where forces are at work that affect and direct our lives.

'God is spirit', says the Scripture, and it might be good for us to get back into the habit of thinking about just what that means. The Bible tells us that before he even created human beings he created *spiritual* beings, called angels. There are almost 300 references to either angels or angelic visitations throughout the Bible.

They are created by God not as something nice for us to put on the front of Christmas cards or trees, but to be – as they are called in the Bible – 'ministering spirits' (see Hebrews 1:14). They exist to serve us, to communicate to us at certain key times as well as to protect us when things sometimes get a little shaky.

Angels are invisible as they don't possess physical bodies, although they appear to human beings every now and then, often taking a physical form. What's more, despite the fact that we may not see them every day, they are hardly what you would call an endangered species. Hebrews 12:22 mentions 'thousands upon thousands' of them.

They were created – just as we were created – and so are not meant to be worshipped. They exist to serve God as well as us. They are not to be confused with the Holy Spirit – he is God, after all – despite the fact that they often appear to be carrying out God's wishes, much in the same way that some have characterised the Holy Spirit.

They appear throughout both the Old and the New Testament, which both have some absolutely classic examples of angelic intervention and interaction with humans. When he was shoved in the lion's den, Daniel found himself joined by an angel who 'shut the mouths of the lions' (Daniel 6:22). Then there was the time (you can read about it in Luke 2) when the angel Gabriel appeared to the shepherds and told them not to be afraid. Other angels showed up and started to worship God. The shepherds were, perhaps understandably, petrified.

Throughout the book of Revelation angels play a key role in John's description of heaven. Even though I find the book fairly confusing, there is so much in it that is helpful and inspiring. Through it the new heaven and the new earth seem to come alive, as the angels who have been at God's side doing his will are going to be joined in their worship by us.

The difference between angels and us is that while we both are created beings, it was into us that God breathed his breath. That means he gave us something of himself, that we have been made in his image and likeness. That's why we and we alone are redeemed and can be called the children of God. We've been adopted and are his offspring. Angels – on the other hand – are simply God's creation, not his children. When God created them he created something outside of himself, like making a computer, a piece of art or a building. They are inspiring and impressive, but ultimately they serve a function. When God created us it was more like giving birth.

There have been plenty of reports in recent times of people having seen angels. Some have seen them just the once while others have notched up a few glimpses. Often it seems that people see them as they are ministering to us, helping us out. I'm sure that this is what they are doing most of the time, and that for various reasons it is us who don't see them rather than them who aren't playing a part in our lives. I think that it's right that we spend most of our time ignorant of their deeds and assistance. They are not there to be worshipped or even noticed; their role is to get God noticed.

When it comes down to it, there are some key truths that lie behind the subject of angels, as well as behind the afterlife and the Second Coming of Jesus. We can take a highly dispassionate stance, approaching in study with a mind to fit it all in to our own parameters of logic and reasoning. We can bend the forces of God to try and fit the rules of rational thought. Unfortunately it never truly satisfies and, after all, what kind of God would he be if we could so easily explain and define, predict and comprehend? In the end the whole point about looking at the subject of life after death is to realise that it is filled with Jesus. Eternal life makes no sense unless not only viewed alongside his life but through his words, through his eyes. Sometimes we humans have latched on to a desire to live for ever, to shrug off the weakness of mortality and emerge from the chrysalis of humanity. From the ancient legends about the elixir of life to the contemporary possibilities offered by drugs and oxygen tanks, the idea has captured the attention of almost every generation. But you know, we make a mess of this life, time and time again. As much as we may crave immortality, we have a natural talent for imposing horror and oppression on our fellow humans. The nightmares that punctuated the twentieth century were not unusual – genocide, greed and godlessness appeared in every century that went before it. Left to our own devices the chances are they'll crop up in the ones that follow it too. Who wants to live for ever when this is the best we can do? Who wants an eternity of greed, corruption and hatred? Sure, we might get better, but get better at what? Refine the ways of practising our sin, hone the ability to turn our backs on God?

As Christians we believe that God – the ultimate higher power – can put things right. We also believe that he has set aside a time for each of us as well as for the planet when life as we know it will come to an end. Replacing it will be a time when 'the lion will lie down with the lamb', when all the wars, pain and misery will cease. At that time we will be so caught up with the Father and his Son that we will join with the angels and the twenty-four elders of Revelation. That's when we will live and reign with him for ever. At the end of the Bible it says 'Amen. Come, Lord Jesus' (Revelation 22:20). Those are the words that we need to be echoing. We need to be praying for Jesus to come back and end this pain and suffering, to come in power and rule with justice, toppling the wicked and destructive. As we live our life here on earth in the light of heaven, becoming increasingly heavenly-minded, we will find for ourselves a whole series of earthly uses of which we never had a clue before. I believe that the thing that God is calling us to do in these days is to go deeper into him. As his people in the West we're so busy doing things that we have forgotten that in the end it's all about finding him, pursuing a relationship with him like a dog after his master. It's about resting in him, worshipping him and placing him above everything else that screams for our attention.

Whenever God's people have tried to get closer to him, reaching a new place of intimacy with their Creator, they have always encountered opposition. Sometimes it has even come from within the family of God, but certainly it has not been unusual for it to come from outside. When you think of King David being so excited at bringing the Ark of the Covenant back into Jerusalem that he danced before the Lord with all his might, there was his wife Michal despising his foolishness. 'Oh, yeah?' he replied. 'And I'll become even more undignified than this.' He refused to let his passion for God be diluted by someone who failed to understand exactly what it meant to him.

In the Gospels we read about Mary, sitting at Jesus' feet, listening to him while her sister Martha kept herself busy in the kitchen. 'Why don't you tell Mary to give us a hand?' Martha asked Jesus. He had to explain how she herself had become distracted and had missed the point of it all; the best thing is to hang out with him. Everything flows out of the relationship.

There's a hymn that we used to sing at school:

> Immortal, invisible, God only wise,
> In light inaccessible hid from our eyes,
> Most blessed, most glorious, the Ancient of
> Days,
> Almighty, victorious, thy great name we
> praise

OK, so the language might seem a tad out of place in the twenty-first century, but the sentiment is timeless, as well as being something that we perhaps have lost. The sense of God's wonder, his otherness, his size. It is as we get a glimpse of eternity that we become fully fit to serve in this life. When we take time to explore the eternal God of heaven, invisible as he is, things change for us. There's an amazing part in the Gospel of John when Jesus prays: 'Now this is eternal life: that they may know you, the only true God, and Jesus Christ whom you have sent' (John 17:3). That's the definition of eternal life; the more we get to know Jesus, the more we get to know heaven. The more we know Jesus, the more we live in the kingdom. The more we live with Jesus in the present, the more we get a glimpse of the future.

That's why worship should take such a high priority in our life here on earth. Worship is the activity of heaven; intimate relationship with God. That's our timetable for eternity. Worship. Worship. More worship. Heaven is going to be saturated with the power, love and goodness of Jesus. Our response will be to love him for it. Fear not though, heaven will not be an eternal church service, it will be unlike anything we have known. We simply will not be able to help ourselves as the passion inside will force its way out as we give God his worth. I'm sure we'll have things to do in heaven – all to do with ruling over the new heaven and the new earth – but it's all going to come from the base of our relationship with God. He created us for himself and for ever he

will have us for himself. Our heart's true home is
him.

'The gift of God is
eternal life, not the gift from God,
as if eternal life were a present
given by God: it is Himself.'
Oswald Chambers

'Aim at heaven
and you will get earth
thrown in. Aim at earth and
you will get neither.'
C.S. Lewis

'We shall not sit on
wispy clouds playing harps,
but we shall have good, fruitful,
satisfying activity. We shall
perfectly, at last — serve him.'
David Winter, *What Happens after Death*

Also by Mike Pilavachi with Craig Borlase

Live the Life
A Soul Survivor Guide to Doing It

It's easy enough being Christians in church or
at Christian events, but how do we even begin to
live the life when we're back home, at college
or at work?

LIVE THE LIFE helps us get to grips with the key
issues that challenge us all:

- How do we deal with temptation and guilt?
- Can we hear God speak?
- How can we share our faith?
- What happens when we worship?
- How can we find God in our weakness and
  failure?
- Can prayer be part of our lifestyle?
- How do we know what to do with our lives?

LIVE THE LIFE doesn't pretend that being a Christian
is easy, but points the way to a walk with God that
impacts the whole of our lives.

*'Working on our relationship with God is the
most valuable thing we can do. LIVE THE LIFE
is going to be a great help to anyone wanting
to go deeper.'* DELIRIOUS?

Hodder & Stoughton
ISBN 0 340 71385 2

Also by Mike Pilavachi with Craig Borlase

For the Audience of One
The Soul Survivor Guide to Worship

Worship is great: the music, the dance . . . but
isn't there more to it than that? Does God enjoy
it as much as we do? What happens when
the music stops?

Worship is not something we do for our own
benefit. It is for God, the audience of one. We
should be worshipping every minute of every day,
and we don't need words or even a tune.

Soul Survivor is at the heart of the incredible revival
in contemporary youth worship. FOR THE AUDIENCE
OF ONE shows that, beneath the surface level of
words and music, a phenomenal work of God –
anointed, culturally relevant and biblically sound –
is taking place, enabling people to be broken,
healed and transformed by him.

It should be read by everyone with a desire to go
deeper in their worship, and includes a special
section for worship leaders.

*'I've hung around Pilavachi for a long time now,
and learnt a load about worship from him.
Read this book and you'll find out effort-free
everything it's taken me ten years to get out
of him!'* MATT REDMAN?

Hodder & Stoughton
ISBN 0 340 72190 1

By David Westlake

Upwardly Mobile
How to Live a Life of Significance

There's more than one way of getting yourself upwardly mobile.

The glossy mags will give you all the advice you need for a fast-track route to flash cars, crisp suits and a seat on the board. But God's blueprint for life has rather different goals: feeding the hungry, sheltering the poor and loosening the chains of injustice.

It's not quite as difficult as it first sounds. You don't need money, power or fame to become a person of significance in God's eyes. UPWARDLY MOBILE will help you discover your potential to make a real difference in the world in which we live.

UPWARDLY MOBILE is the first book by David Westlake, youth director of Tearfund. He has written it with the able assistance of freelance writer Craig Borlase, and publishes it in association with Soul Survivor.

Hodder & Stoughton
ISBN 0 340 75654 3

By Beth Redman

Soul Sista
How to be a Girl of God!

Ever get the feeling . . .

- you spend most of your life trying to be someone you don't really want to be?
- there are too many boys in the world, and not enough men?
- being a Christian shouldn't be half as difficult as everyone tells you it is?
- you want to know God, but you're not sure if he wants to know you?

It's time to fight back! SOUL SISTA is the definitive survival guide for every girl who's ever wondered why the holy life sometimes seems to be just one bad hair day after another. It's about becoming a Girl of God: proud to be a Christian, proud to be a woman.

Beth Redman is an evangelist and schools worker, and former member of the World Wide Message Tribe. She is married to singer and songwriter Matt Redman.

Hodder & Stoughton
ISBN 0 340 75677 2